This Just So story belongs to:

_____

_____

Your name goes here!

This story tells how the armadillo came to be. The tortoise and the hedgehog lived on the banks of the river, escaping the hungry jaguar by swimming away or curling up into a spiky ball. They decided to share their skills with each other to protect themselves from the jaguar, so the hedgehog's prickles became armour like a shell, and the tortoise's shell grew flexible. They called this new animal 'armadillo'!

Rudyard Kipling, born in 1865 in what was then Bombay, India, grew up in love with everything about the country of India: the culture, the people, and the language. He began writing short stories inspired by his time in India, and in 1894 published his famous novel, *The Jungle Book*. The *Just So* stories began as Kipling's bedtime stories for his daughter Effie, and explain the various fantastic and strange ways animals came to look how they do today.

© 2020 North Parade Publishing Ltd.
5 North Parade,
Bath BA1 1LF, UK
www.nppbooks.co.uk

The Beginning
of the
ARMADILLOS

Retold from the Rudyard Kipling original
Illustrated by Ela Jarzabek

Long, long ago, a Stickly-Prickly Hedgehog lived on the banks of the Amazon, eating shelly snails and things.

His friend, the Slow-and-Steady Tortoise, lived nearby, and he ate leafy lettuces and things, and all was well between them.

One day, a Painted Jaguar came to live on the banks of the Amazon too, and he ate everything he possibly could. When he couldn't catch a deer or a monkey for his supper, he ate frogs and beetles instead, and when he couldn't catch frogs or beetles, he went to his Mother Jaguar, who told him how to eat hedgehogs and tortoises.

"When you find a hedgehog you must drop him into the water so that he uncoils" she said. "And when you catch a tortoise you must scoop him out of his shell with your paw!"

The Painted Jaguar thought this very clever, and was pleased that he would never have to miss his supper again.

That evening, he came upon the Stickly-Prickly Hedgehog and the Slow-and-Steady Tortoise.

Stickly-Prickly curled himself up in to a ball, because he was a Hedgehog, and Tortoise drew his head and his feet into his shell, because he was a Tortoise.

"Now, listen to me," said the Painted Jaguar, "because this is important. My mother said that when I meet a Hedgehog I must drop him in the water and then he will uncoil, and when I meet a Tortoise I must scoop him out of his shell with my paw.

"But which of you is a Hedgehog and which is a Tortoise? To save my spots I can't tell!"

"Are you sure of what your Mummy told you?" asked the Stickly-Prickly Hedgehog. "Perhaps she said that when you uncoil a Tortoise you must shell him out of the water with a scoop, and when you paw a Hedgehog you must drop him on the shell?"

"I don't think it was like that at all!" said the Painted Jaguar, but he was puzzled all the same.

"Or perhaps she said that when you water a Hedgehog you must drop him onto your paw, and when you meet a Tortoise you must shell him until he uncoils?" suggested the Slow-and-Steady Tortoise.

"You're making my spots ache!" moaned the Jaguar.

"I don't want your advice at all; I just want to know which of you is a Hedgehog and which is a Tortoise!"

"I shan't tell you!" squeaked the Prickly. "Why don't you try scooping me out of my shell, and see?"

"Aha!" said the Painted Jaguar. "Now I know you're a Tortoise!"

With that, he put out his *paddy-paw* to scoop the
Stickly-Prickly, and, of course, was at once *stickled* with *prickles!*

So shocked was the Painted Jaguar that he knocked the Stickly-
Prickly away.

He rolled away as fast as he could; *straight* into the woods and
bushes where it was far too dark to find him.

"Now I know he wasn't a Tortoise!" said the Painted Jaguar sadly, nursing his paddy-paw. He turned to Slow-and-Steady Tortoise.

"And how do I know for sure what you are?" he wailed.

"I am a Tortoise," said Slow-and-Steady. "And your mother was quite right. You must scoop me out of my shell."

"That's not what you told me a moment ago!" said the Painted Jaguar, sucking the prickles out of his paddy-paw. "You said she said something quite different! And now you say that you want me to scoop you out of your shell!"

"I said nothing of the sort!" snapped the Tortoise. "I said that your mother said that you should scoop me out of my shell, and that is quite different."

"What will happen if I do?" sniffed the Jaguar sulkily.

"I don't know, because I've never been scooped," said Tortoise, "but I'll tell you this for sure: if you want to see me swim away, drop me into the water."

"I don't believe it!" stormed the Jaguar. "You've mixed up all the things my mother said, and now I'm chasing my tail! I was supposed to drop one of you in the water, and now you want to be dropped, which makes me think that you don't want to be dropped at all. So now I am going to drop you!"

"Your mother won't be pleased!" said Slow-and-Steady. "Don't say I didn't warn you!"

With that, the Jaguar dropped the Tortoise into the Amazon, where he swam and swam until he came to a far away bank where the Stickly-Prickly was waiting for him.

"Phew!" said Stickly Prickly. "That was a very narrow escape! I don't like the Painted Jaguar at all. What did you tell him you were?"

"I told him truthfully that I am a Tortoise, but he didn't believe me and dropped me into the river!" explained the Slow-and-Steady.

Just then, from a far away bank, they heard the Painted Jaguar crying to his Mummy about what he'd done that he shouldn't have done.

"And now I haven't got anything to eat at all!" he wailed.

"Hush, my son!" said Mother Jaguar gently. "A Tortoise can't curl himself up. By this you can spot a Tortoise."

"I don't like this lady one bit!" said the Slow-and-Steady. "I wonder what else she knows?"

"A hedgehog can curl himself up" Mother Jaguar went on, "and his prickles stick out every which way at once. By this you may know a Hedgehog."

"Even Painted Jaguar can't forget that!" cried Stickly-Prickly. And sure enough, from far away on the banks of the Amazon, they heard the Painted Jaguar singing happily to himself:

'Can't curl, but can swim--
Slow-Steady, that's him!
Curls up, but can't swim--
Stickly-Prickly, that's him!'

"I must learn to swim," cried Stickly-Prickly "can you teach me? I can help you learn to curl up too!"

"Excellent!" said Slow-and-Steady, and he held up Stickly-Prickly's chin while the little Hedgehog splashed and flailed in the waters of the Amazon and Stickly-Prickly helped to unlace Tortoise's back-plates, so that he could twist and turn and bend about.

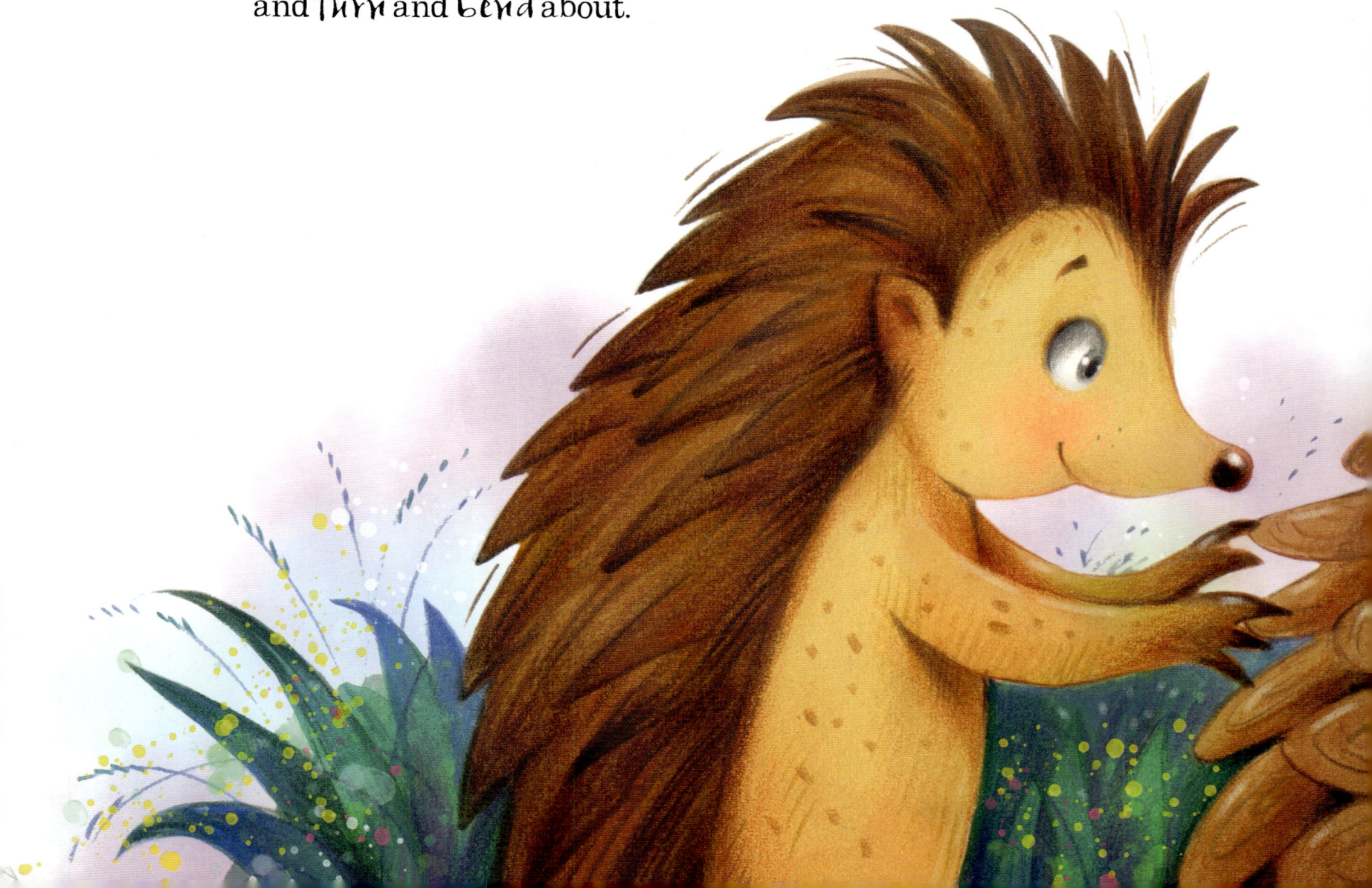

And so the two friends *practiced* and *practiced*, until Stickly-Prickly could swim without splashing and Slow-and-Steady could curl up without grunting with effort.

By and by, Stickly-Prickly noticed that Slow-and-Steady had strained his back plates a little, so that they were *overlapping*, instead of lying side-by-side.

At the same time, Slow-and-Steady noticed that Stickly-Prickly's prickles were all *melting* in to one another.

"You look more like a pinecone, now!" he said. "You used to look like a chestnut-burr!"

They went on with their exercises, each helping the other, until morning came, and by first light they saw that they were both quite different from how they had been before.

"Won't Painted Jaguar be surprised!" they cried as they looked at each other. "Let's go and find him!"

And find him they did, still nursing his paddy-paw by the banks of the Amazon.

He was so astonished to see them that he fell three times backwards over his painted tail!

"Good morning!" said Stickly-Prickly, who was no longer stickly and prickly.

"Good morning" said Painted Jaguar. "Forgive me; I do not remember your name?"

"That's unkind of you," said Stickly-Prickly, "seeing as only last night you tried to scoop me out of my shell with your paw!"

"But you didn't have a shell before!" said Painted Jaguar, confused. "It was all prickles! Just look at my paw!" And sure enough, Stickly-Prickly's prickles were still sticking and prickling in the Jaguar's paddy-paw.

"You dropped me into the Amazon to be drowned!" piped up Slow-and-Steady. "I'm surprised that you can't remember either of us today!" and laughing, they sang:

"Can't curl, but can swim--
Slow-Steady, that's him!
Curls up, but can't swim--
Stickly-Prickly, that's him!"

With that, the two friends curled themselves up into balls and rolled round and round, before diving into the Amazon for a swim.

Painted Jaguar was so confused that his eyes turned cart-wheels in his head!

Can you guess what he did next?

He went to fetch his mother!

"Can't curl, but can swim--
Slow-Steady, that's him!
Curls up, but can't swim--
Stickly-Prickly, that's him!"